# Cara's Journey Home

## A Parable for Today's Woman

*For Sheila Waters,
With appreciation
for your wonderful
calligraphy.
Blessings,
Catherine Monserrat*

## Catherine Monserrat, Ph.D.

*37 Herrada Rd. Santa Fe NM 87508*

Infinite Options
Santa Fe, New Mexico

Copyright 2002 by Catherine Monserrat, Ph.D.

ISBN 0-9723811-0-4

*Cara's Journey Home* is a work of fiction. All characters, events, and dialogues are fictitious, and any resemblance to real people and circumstances is purely coincidental and does not change the fictitious nature of the work.

Published by:
Infinite Options
7 Avenida Vista Grande, #221
Santa Fe, New Mexico 87508-8199

Cover Design: Kim D'Angelo, Bookcovers.com
Decorative Double Capitals: Sheila Waters, 1978. Reproduced by permission.
Author Photo: Kim Jew Photography Studio

For
Bernardo,
Debbie and Glenn
I dedicate this story to you
and to my grandchildren.

# Table of Contents

# Introduction

Cara first came into being at a writers' retreat some five years ago. After the workshop, I went home and promptly forgot about her. Then, last summer, she popped back into my head, her story longing to be written. At the time, I was busy, too busy to think about writing anything. But the tale persistently re-entered my thoughts, while driving to work, trying to go to sleep at night, in the middle of a novel.

Finally, I gave in. I realized that this was not "my" story. It was a story for women, a gift to them. So, I settled back and enjoyed the process, literally waiting to see what would happen next. People who write fiction frequently describe this experience; how characters show up and define themselves, how tales unfold. Having never written fiction, I was taken by surprise.

As a therapist and educator, I have been privileged to witness the unfolding lives of many people. I can attest to the fact that every woman's journey is unique, every tale worthy of recognition. Yet, underneath the uniqueness, there are common themes that weave through the fabric of women's lives.

Myths, parables and fairy tales have been told throughout history as a means of exploring these themes. *Cara's Journey Home* is that kind of tale. Obviously, it is not intended as a "how to" book or a model for behavior. However, it does provide an opportunity to visit the universal themes and reflect on the ways they appear in our own lives. Cara is not intended to represent a particular woman or all women, any more than was Cinderella, Sleeping Beauty or Ariel. Likewise, Broen does not embody every man. Neither did Prince Charming, the Seven Dwarfs or Merlin. All of the characters in the story are symbolic of the deeper themes that impact our lives, various aspects of our personalities and the paradoxes with which we all struggle. It is in that spirit that I offer Cara's story to you. May her journey inspire your own.

# The Beginning

nce upon a time, in a land of beauty and peace, there dwelled a farmer known as Colin. He was a tall, brawny sort of man, the kind who could give you a start because he appeared to be so powerful. Yet, on closer examination, his eyes were soft and a smile played timidly at the corners of his mouth. Those who were acquainted with him could tell you that he was kind and strong and generous. Few knew Colin really well, because he was quiet and tended to keep to himself. Many a young woman had attempted to catch his eye, but he seemed completely unaware of their interest. In this way, they thought him strange, because he truly appeared satisfied living alone, working with his animals and tending his crops. After a time, most of the village girls accepted that Colin would always be a bachelor.

This farmer was also quite prosperous for a man who worked his own plot of land. Every weekend during the times of harvest, he loaded his old wagon and took his produce to the market in the neighboring town. His booth was always swamped, because matrons and servants alike knew he would treat them fairly and sell them the best that he had. Many of the younger women would linger, pretending to ponder their choices, but secretly hoping to be noticed. Colin, ever friendly, showed them all the same quiet kindness.

Until finally, one day, he looked up from his crates directly into the green eyes of a lovely young woman. He was sure he'd never seen her before. She stared at him frankly, something that both excited and unnerved him. They did not speak and to his dismay, she left suddenly without purchasing anything. Colin wondered who this remarkable woman might be, as he thought he knew everyone who frequented the market. He found it curious that her clothing seemed expensive and so beautifully tailored, unusual dress for women in this marketplace. By asking a few questions, he learned that her name was Selene and that she was the daughter of a wealthy landholder who indulged her every whim. The gossip was that she had been sneaking out with the maid on market days as a remedy for her increasing sense of boredom. Upon learning about the young woman's status, Colin immediately decided to put her out of his mind. It was not at all wise for a commoner to show an interest in a woman of wealth!

Selene was also quite taken with the young farmer. The rumors were true. She was suffering from a horrible boredom, trapped in the monotony of her privileged lifestyle. She felt exhilarated, rebellious and free as she contemplated a forbidden flirtation. So in the ensuing weeks, she found excuses to accompany the maid to market. Each time she met the farmer, she became more and more forward, smiling, laughing and engaging him in conversation. Inevitably, he was smitten. Over time, their desire blossomed as they found opportunities to meet without being discovered. Finally, they made the decision that they must be together.

Colin, in good faith, went to Selene's father to ask for her hand in marriage. Her father was enraged and threw the young man out of his home, threatening his life should he ever see his daughter again. He fired the maid and confined Selene to the house. Colin, humiliated and brokenhearted, returned to his farm. Despite his sorrow, he realized that their relationship was hopeless and that he must find a way to go on without his love. He wondered how he had allowed such a thing to happen in the first place. Hadn't he known better?

Selene was not so easily discouraged. She couldn't get the young farmer off her mind. The more she longed for him, the more she wanted him. For weeks, she plotted her escape, and early one morning she appeared on Colin's doorstep. She pleaded with him to let her stay. She swore that she could not bear to live without him, even if it meant forsaking her family.

Even as this was happening, Selene was experiencing some doubts. In truth, she had been startled when the coach stopped in front of Colin's tiny cottage. The woman could scarcely believe her eyes. The gray stone house was little more than an outbuilding. And the farm was so small! The entire village was not as big as the vast floral gardens on the estate from which she had come! She swallowed hard, trying to mask her disappointment, and silently squinted across the narrow pasture. "Well," she thought to herself, "it matters not how much land there is. I know my beloved is beautiful and loving and that he will take wonderful care of me. I will be very happy here and will enjoy the spacious home that he will build for me once we are wed."

Colin was overjoyed when Selene had arrived at his door that morning. The couple was soon wed and, for a few months, they were very happy. The villagers were cordial to the young woman, often dropping by with gifts of food and flowers from their gardens. Selene always politely thanked them, but with a voice laced with the condescension of one who had been accustomed to the care of servants.

At first, the young bride enjoyed the little farmhouse, but constantly talked about the large home she wanted her new husband to build. He assured her that one day, when his profits increased, they would add other rooms. Secretly, though, he worried whether that day would ever come. He was already the most successful farmer in his village and doubted that his small plot would ever become the grand farm that his wife had envisioned.

As time wore on, the woman grew restless. The newness of her marriage gave way to a tedium that she found intolerable. Her husband arose early every morning and was often gone before she awakened. In the evenings, he would return tired, hungry and dirty. She would have spent the day preening for him, but he seemed to take little notice. This angered her, as did his obvious expectation that she should do chores around the house. Chores! She was not a woman born to chores! She was a woman who was born to comfort and to managing a household of servants. Gradually, the farmer came to realize that his wife, while as captivating as he had dreamed, was spoiled and had an unpleasant disposition. No matter how hard he tried, she was never satisfied. Even so, he loved her and did all he could to make a life that would bring her comfort.

When Selene realized she was with child, she was horrified. How could they take care of a child when they had no servants and such a small house? Who would feed and bathe the baby? She couldn't possibly have a child without a nanny. She cried continuously from morning till night, hoping that somehow her resistance would make her condition go away. But the truth was clear. She was going to bear a child in these deplorable conditions.

Selene's pregnancy went well. Nonetheless, she constantly bemoaned her plight, complaining about every change in her body. She blamed her husband for the terrible tragedy that had befallen her, and they became even more distanced during those months. Secretly Colin was delighted, as he had always enjoyed children. So, despite his wife's wailing, he looked after her with great care and anticipated the birth with quiet enthusiasm. Surely, once the little one was born, Selene would share in his delight.

When her time came, Selene was attended by the skillful village midwife, and the birth was amazingly easy. The baby was a girl, whom they called Cara. Colin was immediately enchanted by his little daughter. Selene, relieved to no longer be pregnant, merely tolerated the child. Selene was almost completely without mothering instincts and gave the child minimal care during the day. At night, Colin would come home and eagerly take the baby in his arms. During those evening hours, he would cuddle her, talk with her, bathe her and marvel at her beauty. He tried to help his wife see what a miraculous little girl they had been given. But Selene would just turn away from them both, looking pale and drawn. In truth, she was terribly homesick, longing to return to her family, to the ease and familiarity of her upbringing.

After a few short months, the young mother could no longer tolerate her situation. She took a last look at her sleeping infant and left as she had come, stealing away in the night in the company of her father's servant. Colin, though brokenhearted, did not follow her. He understood her unhappiness and knew that he could never offer Selene the kind of life to which she aspired. She belonged back in the care of her family, living the life of privilege for which she had been bred.

# A Gift is Revealed

espite his grief at the loss of his wife, the farmer settled into a life of greater peace. He continued to work the field by day and to enjoy fatherhood in the evenings. The woman from the neighboring farm had six small children of her own and was more than willing to care for Cara during the day. And, so, life took on a natural pace for Colin and his little child.

Fortunately, Cara had her father's wonderful temperament. Although a bit quiet, she was an energetic, happy child.

During the day, she was surrounded by the laughter and attention of the children and the loving warmth of her "Auntie." As the sun would begin to set, she would watch for the solid figure of her father, coming up the road in his old wagon to fetch her. Colin's arrival was always the highlight of her day. It had been for as long as she could remember.

As the little girl grew, her father taught her all about the farm. She loved to help plant the seeds in the spring and help with the harvest in the fall. But her greatest passion was tending the animals. She helped feed them and made sure they had fresh water. At times, when her animals were injured or sick, she would hold them like babies and make soft crooning sounds. While her father found this behavior somewhat strange, he never interfered. Often the animals under her care would recover! He knew his little daughter was somewhat unusual in this regard, so he seldom discussed it with others.

In spite of his caution, the word began to get out among the villagers that Cara had a unique ability to work with animals and help them recover when they were ill. No one really remembered when the townsfolk first began to bring their pets and livestock to her for healing. It didn't really matter to them that she was strange or that she made odd crooning sounds when she held an animal. What mattered was that Cara had gained a reputation for being able to restore health to the sick and injured creatures that were brought to her.

When Cara was a teenager, an event occurred that would suddenly and irreversibly alter the course of her life. She and her father were both sleeping soundly, when they were awakened in the middle of the night to the sounds of loud crying. Someone was pounding on their door, calling for help. The visitors were acquaintances from a neighboring hamlet. In their arms was a tiny infant, obviously very sick. The child's face was flushed and burning hot to the touch. Their village elder had told them that their tiny girl was gravely ill and would die before the week was up. He had sent them home with instructions for keeping the little one comfortable during her last hours. The parents, desperate for any shred of hope, had traveled to see if Cara's healing touch and crooning sounds might restore the child in some way. They had nothing to lose. Would she please, please offer their little one some of her comfort?

Cara and her father exchanged puzzled glances. This situation had them both startled. It was one thing to care for sickly animals, but a human infant? Almost before she could think, Cara took the tiny baby in her arms and carried her over to the chair by the fire. She held the baby and began to croon. The others stood aside, watching and waiting. The crooning went on for hours. Cara crooned and rocked and rocked and crooned. She spoke to the little one in reassuring tones. Colin and the frightened parents simply stood by and watched. They knew that, at the very least, Cara's healing touch was calming the little girl. In fact, the child's breathing grew less labored, and she appeared less flushed.

After two days in Cara's arms, the baby began to revive. She was able to take small amounts of nourishment and seemed to respond to the voices and faces around her. Finally, Cara told the parents she had done all she could. They could take the baby home. Both she and Colin wished the family well and sent them on their way. As it turned out, the baby lived and thrived, and Cara's reputation as a healer began to spread throughout the land.

It became customary for people to bring their children to Cara for treatment. Then they began to bring the elderly as well. No one understood exactly what it was that she did, least of all Cara herself. But her work in helping with the sick became legendary. While her father toiled in the field during the day, Cara received visits from those in need of her care. The villagers paid her with food and handmade garments and even coins. She and her father began to prosper in ways that they had never dreamed possible.

And so their life went, happily and peacefully in the little village. The days passed into months, the months into years, and Cara became a young woman. Colin purchased a horse and carriage so that she could visit people's homes when they were too ill to come to her.

As it turned out, the midwife was aging and needed help. She invited Cara to accompany her as she attended the women during childbirth. Seeing that the girl had an aptitude for the work, she made her an apprentice. Cara was an eager learner and gained confidence as they worked side by side. Under the midwife's guidance, she began to use herbs that she grew in her garden to help relieve the symptoms of common illnesses. Cara was doing what came naturally, and she was happy.

# The Cycles of Life

Gradually, Cara's father began to lose stamina. He tired more easily and came in from the fields long before sunset. And he slept past sunrise most mornings. He did not appear to be unhappy, but he was failing. A quiet man, he had never openly expressed his doubts about Cara's future. Now, he began to address his concerns. He did not trust that her healing work could adequately support her and was worried that she would not be able to survive without him. In short, he felt Cara needed a husband.

Cara was surprised to learn of Colin's doubts. She knew that she was different than the other women, and she had never had a suitor. Yet, she refused to be worried, fully expecting that her father would recover and that all would continue as before. Cara nursed him with great kindness and joy. She could not accept that her beloved father might be dying.

One day, without warning, the farmer did not awaken. Cara was thrown into a darkness such as she had never known. A life without her father was unthinkable! She withdrew from the world, refusing to see patients and wandering aimlessly around the empty house. The villagers, seeing Cara's plight, paid visits and offered their support. Occasionally, she would let them in. More often, she would not answer the door. Finally, the women began to leave food outside her door, and the men quietly came to tend the farm and to make minor repairs. Out of respect, they left her to her grief.

One morning, there was a resounding knock on the front door. Still in her dressing gown, Cara lifted her head, her dull reverie thus interrupted. She glanced with mild interest at her surroundings. Far too untidy to admit any visitors, she thought. Best to ignore them in silence and allow them to slip away. But the visitor was persistent, and the knocking repeated itself again. And again.

Finally, a voice called out, "Miss Cara! Miss Cara? I know you are in there. We've come such a long way to see you. Please open the door now. Miss Cara, it is me! Adele, from the neighboring hamlet. Don't you remember Adele, whose baby girl you saved from death's door? And as a surprise, I have brought her with me. She's a healthy, sparkling little girl. Surely, you want to see her!"

Cara sat up straight, caught in the memory of the fragile infant whom she had nursed those many hours. Yes, she thought. Yes, I would like to see this child, very much.

"Oh, yes, I do remember you, Adele, and your baby! Please wait one moment. I am afraid I was just dressing. Make yourselves comfortable on the porch."

Cara raced to the mirror and, to her dismay, the reflection was even worse than she had feared. She looked like a hag, her hair dirty and tangled, her face grimy. She quickly brushed her hair and grabbed the cleanest dress she could find. On the way to the door, she pulled an apron from a hook, hoping it would camouflage the wrinkled garment.

Cara opened the door, revealing Adele's beaming face. Next to her, holding her hand, was a pixie of a girl with an identical smile. The little girl enthusiastically thrust a bouquet of wild flowers into Cara's hand. Cara accepted the gift and knelt down so that she was eye level with the child. "Well, thank you for that wonderful gift! And what is the name of this big girl who has brought these beautiful flowers?"

"I am Anna Cara!" the toddler exclaimed proudly. "And I am almost four years old!"

"Well, it is certainly a pleasure to meet you, Anna Cara. Please come in, both of you."

Adele surveyed the disarray of the cottage and, hiding her alarm, said brightly, "I think the two of you should sit down and get acquainted! I will make tea. Now Anna Cara, this is Cara, for whom you were named! Remember? At bedtime, we tell the story of how she held you as a baby."

"Oh yes," replied Anna Cara with clarity beyond her tender years. "I was very sick and you helped me get better."

Cara was stunned by all the information that was coming her way. A child named for her? A child now four? The family incorporating Cara into their bedtime stories? A lump formed in her throat.

The child did not seem to notice at all and chattered on. "My mama says you have animals. Can I see them? Are there baby animals? Can I hold them? I would be careful. Do you have eggs we could gather? Can we go out now?"

Cara's aching heart was soothed by the salve of the child's spirit. Before too long, they were venturing outside, hand in hand, to meet the animals. Adele watched them with relief, choosing to stay inside and do what she could to put order to the chaos. The truth was that she had heard of Cara's plight and had come with full intention of doing all she could to remedy the situation. She planned to stay until it was clear that Cara was doing better.

The mother and daughter remained with Cara for many days. By the end of the visit, they had all become fast friends. Under their care, Cara had regained some of her energy. When the time came for the two to return home, Cara vowed to her namesake that she would visit them soon and that there would be many more happy days spent on the farm with the animals. The delighted child threw her arms around Cara in parting and whispered, "I do so love you. I will be back."

That was the beginning of Cara's recovery. With the coming of spring, she felt a renewed sense of aliveness. Although she still missed her father, she ventured out of the house and resumed her care of the animals. Village women again called on her to attend their births. Without Colin to care for, she was able to devote all of her energies to her healing work. She worked by day and studied at night, learning about new herbs and making notes in her log. The old midwife died, so she was called to attend all of the births in the region and to hold vigils with the dying. Again, Cara found herself expressing the fullness of her gifts.

Actually, the young woman's work life was rich and deeply satisfying. She needed nothing. The villagers saw to that. But at night, after a long hard day, she would find herself lonely. She longed for the joviality of conversation she had shared with her father. She missed having meals with him and sharing stories of their day. Because she worked so hard, she had never made friends with the other young women her age. Besides, when she was in their company, she felt out of place, having little in common with them. Most of her peers were now married, with children. Cara herself had stood at their sides for the births. And, so, she spent her evenings alone in the safety of her cottage, wishing for friendly companionship, but not knowing where she might find it.

# The Newcomer

That summer, a rumor began to spread among the villagers that a learned man had been traveling around the countryside. It was said that he was a powerful orator and a great teacher. Supposedly, he also had the gift of healing, much like their own Cara. Cara listened to the rumors with a mixture of amusement and curiosity. It would be fun for her to meet someone like herself with whom she could share ideas and trade experiences. Perhaps he might visit their village, and she could spend a bit of time with him.

One day, a traveling salesman arrived announcing that he had encountered the young scholar on the road the previous day. He expounded upon the man's powerful voice and extraordinary wisdom. Their village would be lucky, he said, if this special man came their way. The villagers urged the salesman to invite the orator to visit them. They had one healer in their village already, but she was a woman who was mostly self-taught. How they would love to have the input of a wise one such as he! The salesman said that, if he were to meet the scholar again, he would deliver the invitation.

The village went into an uproar. What if this great one came to visit? What if he might stay? Perhaps he would teach Cara everything he knew and they, the villagers, would benefit from the best wisdom he would bring from far and wide. Cara listened calmly with a smile on her face. Inside, she was as anxious as the rest of them. Indeed, it would be wonderful to have someone with whom to share her work. Since her father's death, she had felt the tremendous burden of living alone and being called upon to serve so many. "Perhaps," she muttered with delight, "we could become true friends."

After a few weeks, the word came. The scholar was nearby and would be arriving at their village very soon. Preparations began in earnest. The townsfolk were concerned that someone of such a reputation would find their village inadequate. So they cleaned and preened and prepared a great feast. Then, they gathered in the square to await the arrival of this amazing being. The young women whispered and giggled among themselves, for it was said that he was handsome and quite marriageable. Perhaps he was even rich! Might he choose a bride from among them?

The townsfolk had so blown his stature and arrival out of proportion that when he actually appeared, there was a mild letdown among the people. He arrived, not in a grand carriage or with an entourage as had been rumored. Actually, he was riding a sorry old nag and was accompanied by two scruffy black dogs. Despite his humble attire and rather common entrance, the young man was extraordinarily handsome and did seem to have a unique presence about him. So, the villagers cheered as he rode into town and surrounded him with shouts of welcome.

Cara stood at the edge of the crowd, quietly observing the commotion. She cared little whether or not this man was wealthy, or whether he arrived with an entourage. In fact, given the stories of her mother's relatives, she had rather hoped he was not of that particular breed. Most of all, Cara wished that he might become a true friend and confidant. She hoped he would help her with her healing work and offer her encouragement and knowledge.

Finally, the village elder made his way through the crowd and spoke to the visitor with a voice of authority. "Fine sir," he said, "we welcome you among us! We are a small village, but we have much to offer for your comfort. Our people are loving, our mountains pristine, and our rivers clear. Our fields give us ample harvest each year. We invite you to stop and spend time with us while we share our bounty. Share your wisdom with us and allow us to welcome you with food and lodging."

"My thanks to you and your townsfolk," he replied. "I am known as Broen. In truth, I am weary from many months of travel. I find your mountains and forests inviting. I will welcome the warmth of your fires and your friendly companionship. I will gladly share all that I know with any who would listen. I hear, too, that there is a renowned healer in your midst, a woman named Cara. I'd be eager to meet one of such a fine reputation. I'd like to match my skills with hers. Perhaps I can teach her a thing or two!"

Cara shrunk back, dismayed by his words. He sounded so arrogant. She felt herself startled by his conceit and frankly repulsed by his attitude. Silently, she slipped out of the crowd and returned to the safety of her cottage. That night, she sat ruminating in front of her fire. "He wants to match skills with me," she mumbled with distaste. "Why must he speak in this way? I've no interest in competing with this man." Gradually, her feelings of anger subsided, only to be replaced by a flood of sadness and disappointment. Oh, she had so hoped that the young scholar would be a friend and companion, a salve for her sense of loneliness and isolation. Obviously, he had wanted to meet her, too, but in the spirit of competition.

For the next few weeks, the villagers thronged to listen to the young man. Broen spoke every day in the Village Square and offered his services in exchange for food and lodging. He was, in fact, capable of wonderful oratory.

He was a moving and charismatic character. Though his flamboyant manner took the villagers aback at times, they soon adapted. After all, they reasoned, such a learned one was entitled to a little smugness. Besides, it was fun to listen to him, compared to the calm, quiet countenance they had always known in Cara. All agreed the young man was a tremendous asset to their village and hoped he could be convinced to stay.

# The Lovers

n spite of his arrogance, Cara found herself somewhat relieved by the scholar's presence in their village. Since childhood, she had been busy caring for the sick ones. Broen's presence provided a much-needed reprieve from her demanding duties. She enjoyed her days of freedom, baking, gardening and singing to herself. While she noticed that the villagers were seeking her services less often, she welcomed the time of leisure. She knew that soon enough he would be on his way, and her life would be as busy as ever.

One day, Cara was startled by a knock at her door. She opened it to find the scholar standing before her holding a bouquet of flowers. "Good day," he smiled. "I have been waiting for you to come visit me or to attend one of my lectures. But since you have not chosen to come to me, I have decided to come to you. I understand that you are the longstanding healer in this village. I am somewhat surprised to learn that you have actually sent people to me for help. They are bringing me gifts of livestock, vegetables and woven garments in payment for my services. Today, I was actually offered a small parcel of land in payment for my work with a sick child. I have come to introduce myself and to express my appreciation to you for your support."

Cara was somewhat taken aback by his friendly, unaffected manner. She invited Broen in and offered him a cup of tea. The two sat at her table in awkward silence. Quite a contrast, she noted, to the wonderful visions she had originally held for their meetings. He began to talk, and she listened in silence. Her heart began to soften toward this young man. For beneath his bravado, he seemed to be quite well meaning and sincere in his desire to be of service. She was surprised to discover that she was enjoying his company and finding his stories interesting.

"I want to thank you for this visit," he said, "and for this opportunity to sit in your company. As you probably understand, my kind of work can feel lonely at times, even though I am often in the company of many people. I do long for conversation with others who share my particular passions. I fear I have talked too much. Perhaps we could spend some time together again, and you can tell me something of your own experiences." With that he stood to leave, and he flashed her an engaging smile.

That night as she lay alone in her bed, Cara reflected on her time with him. Perhaps she had been too hasty, too harsh in her judgments. He had, this very day, offered her a glimpse of the kind of companionship she craved. If she could just look beyond his arrogant manner to what was obviously a good heart, perhaps they could be friends after all.

So gradually, Cara opened her home and then her heart to Broen. Indeed, the two did become the closest of friends. Over the winter months, their visits became more frequent. They would share a meal, a fire and lengthy discussions. There were, of course, a number of girls in the village who suffered disappointment at the rumors that the two were forging a strong friendship. Most of the villagers, far from being jealous or scandalized, were immensely relieved. They had felt guilty for their abandonment of Cara. Now, if she joined forces with Broen, they could have the benefit of both!

In the spring, Broen and Cara announced that they would wed. The villagers were ecstatic. Their beloved Cara had found an ideal mate. Their township would thrive in the safe hands of two such powerful healers. Perhaps their offspring would also carry the healing gifts. Their village would become renowned throughout the land. They would all become wealthy. And what's more, they would never have to fear again.

Often Broen and Cara would talk late into the night about their healing techniques. Cara taught Broen about the use of herbs, and he began to incorporate them into his work. However, he strongly believed that everything could be explained scientifically. He saw no need for the more subtle types of healing. Of course, Cara felt differently. She knew that her crooning and healing touch were related to the heart. For her, the heart was the seat of true healing.

While Broen loved Cara deeply, he considered her ideas strange and, frankly, unscientific. He found his own methods more clear and logical, while hers seemed too soft and unfounded. Over time, his judgments began to influence her thinking. He was, after all, quite effective. She began to entertain doubts about the use of her voice for healing. Perhaps her heart's intuition wasn't real. Broen was probably right.

Cara was happy to be married to Broen. She enjoyed their life together; particularly their long walks in the woods. At the same time, she noticed that she was losing enthusiasm for her own healing work. When people would come to her, she would suggest they see Broen instead.

Cara had great respect for her husband and desperately wanted to please him. So she watched him closely and tried to imitate everything he did. Yet, she found that she lacked confidence and struggled whenever she used his techniques. As a result, she tired easily.

Quite unexpectedly, the villagers received news of a dreadful illness spreading across the land. The townspeople were alarmed. The elders called a meeting to discuss how they would respond if their village was affected. Everyone at the meeting was agitated and fearful, talking at once and shouting out their opinions. Finally, Broen took charge and called them to order. Cara was delighted by the skill with which he managed the situation.

Gradually, the crowd calmed, and the discussion became more specific. The villagers looked to Broen for their answers. Cara, once their greatest authority on health, felt somehow superfluous to the process. Even though she had some ideas to contribute to the plan, she remained quiet and allowed the discussion to go on without her. She was puzzled by her own behavior, yet no one else seemed to notice.

Shortly after that event, Cara completely lost interest in her work and stopped doing it all together. Instead, she devoted herself to the running of the household and the farm. She gardened and baked and enjoyed the quiet freedom of her life at home.

# The Warning

One day, Broen noticed that Cara didn't look well. She had become thin and pale and had darkened circles under her eyes. She still laughed often, but her laughter had a hollow ring. This puzzled Broen. But he was also busy. Since Cara no longer worked with him, he felt the full burden for healing in the village. At times, he was resentful that she was not of more help, and he treated her harshly. Why couldn't she be more helpful? Why couldn't she work beside him and, well.... be more like him?

Late that summer Cara, feeling exceptionally tired, decided to sit in the sun near her garden. Crying quietly, she realized she missed Broen and the joy they had once shared. He was so busy now that he was seldom home. Even more than that, she missed her own healing songs. She missed holding the children, nursing the elderly and helping deliver the babies. Her voice was soft and wispy. Though she hated to admit it to herself, she had completely lost the ability to croon. Sometimes, alone in her garden, she had tried to reclaim her songs. But try as she might, no sounds would come.

Wiping away her tears, Cara glanced at the edge of her garden and was startled to see an old woman standing there. She was puzzled that she had never seen the woman before, since she thought she knew everyone for miles around. Besides, she hadn't heard the woman approach and was embarrassed that this stranger had discovered her crying alone.

"What's wrong with you, Girl?" the old crone inquired. "Why do you sit here wasting your tears? Keep it up and you'll dry out entirely!" The woman's voice was raspy as was common for someone her age, but it was also quite powerful, and she seemed to be genuinely interested. Since Cara was desperately lonely and longing for company, she began to tell the old woman her story. She spoke of her childhood and how she had developed the powers to heal the animals. She told her how she'd used her crooning voice, and how she had loved to heal from her heart. She talked about how she now realized that Broen's techniques were far superior, but how applying them had left her tired and depleted. Finally, she admitted to her isolation without even the comfort of her own voice. The truth was that her life had become empty, bereft of meaning.

The old woman listened quietly. Then she frowned. This situation was grave, far more serious than the girl realized. The crone had seen this wasting illness before, and she understood that it could be deadly. If this young woman didn't regain the use of her voice and ceased offering her gifts to the world, she would surely die.

Not wanting to frighten her, the old woman said, "You must sing again, Dear One. Your heart and soul long to sing. And remember, you have been given a great gift to offer the world. It must not be wasted like this."

"I can't!" exclaimed Cara. "I've tried for months to sing while in my garden. No sound comes out at all. Recently a little sparrow had injured his wing. Always before, I was able to help such a condition. This time, I couldn't comfort him at all. Without my song, he died in my hands." With that, Cara broke into uncontrollable sobs.

The crone leaned heavily on her cane. "Listen to me. Your husband Broen is a wise scholar and wonderful healer. He has tried, but he has been unable to help you. The chances are that he cannot. But there is someone I know who can help you. My sister, Leah. She lives on the other side of the mountain in the Valley of the Bluebells. She has helped many others recover from this kind of illness and to regain their voices. You must go to her at once."

"How would I find her?" asked Cara softly.

"My sister lives across the Great Mountain in a lush valley. The journey is long and hard. You could make it if you leave at once and travel steadily. I warn you, you must leave soon. When the harsh winter snows come, you will not be able to make it across the mountain. Higher up, the trees have already begun to turn to gold. You must make haste. Once with my sister, you can pass the winter in her care and return in the spring."

Cara was astonished. Leave her home for a whole winter? Leave Broen? Travel across the mountains to an unknown land all alone? The prospect seemed overwhelming, quite impossible. "No," she thought. "I will just carry on as I have. Surely things will get better soon."

"Thank you for listening and for your advice, Good Woman," whispered Cara. "I am truly grateful for your concern. While I trust your word, I cannot leave my husband and my home to venture forth in that way. I have never traveled alone. Why, I've barely even left this village! I will take your cautions to heart. I will try every day to recover my voice. And if I do not, it will not be so bad, will it? I still have the comfort of my beautiful garden and the song of the birds."

The old crone was silent for what seemed like an eternity. Then, she spoke. Her voice, though soft and cracked with age, carried great conviction. "The loss of your songs is, indeed, very sad. I have no doubt that you could exist for some time more without them.  But I fear the loss of your voice is a symptom of something far more serious.  If you do not care for yourself, you may perish.  You need rest, to be quiet in the company of my sister and her friends.  You need to drink the tea brewed from the bluebells that grow in the Valley.  Only then can you hope to live in health and joy in the company of your husband."

With that, the old woman handed Cara a map outlining the journey across the mountain.  "I will leave you now," she said.  The crone turned slowly and leaning on her cane, she moved away.  Before Cara could say goodbye, the old woman was gone.

"How on earth did she move so quickly?" Cara asked herself.  She tucked the map in the pocket of her apron and went inside the house to set the fire for the evening.  The woman was right about one thing.  The chill of early fall was indeed in the air!

# The Journey

ry as she might, Cara was unable to erase the old woman's warnings from her mind. "What if I am seriously ill?" she mused. Looking at her reflection in the mirror, it was obvious how thin and pale she had become. Her energies were low, and it was true that she lacked her usual luster. And, oh, she did miss the chance to heal the children and the animals with her gift of sound. She felt so, so hollow inside.

A few days later, Cara awakened with a start. She had been dreaming of her own death. Shaken, she began the business of her day. No matter what she did, the feeling of foreboding remained with her. That evening she attempted to tell Broen about her experience with the old woman and about her concerns over her waning health. He was tired and distracted that particular evening. Normally, he was a good listener, but in his exhaustion, he was more abrupt than usual. He complained that her voice was too soft and that he had to strain himself to hear her. Besides, he thought she was overreacting. Cara was being ridiculous. Things couldn't be that serious. She had a life of ease, one any other woman would envy! Why would she let a crazy old hag influence her like this? Finally, he got up wearily from the table and went to bed, saying that he had another important day tomorrow and needed to rest. They would talk more tomorrow when both of them were feeling better.

For the first time, Cara felt truly afraid. She felt lonely and frightened that Broen had been unable to hear her. She knew he was tired and that they had had similar conversations many times before. The young woman sat at the table, her chin resting heavily on her palms, watching as the fire slowly died. She was unable to sleep. Outside she heard the faraway call of a night owl and the soulful wail of the timber wolf. Always before these sounds had held a familiar comfort, but tonight they filled her with dread. If she were to make the lonely trip to the Valley of the Bluebells she would spend many dark, cold nights alone with sounds such as these. Surprisingly, her alternative seemed even darker. And so in the gloom of the long, sleepless night, Cara decided she would set off on her journey at daybreak.

Broen was up at dawn and rushed out for a meeting with the town's leaders. Feeling the need to explain herself, she wrote him a long letter expressing her deep love and admiration for his greatness. She explained that she was risking this journey in the hope of regaining some of her former vibrancy and healing powers. And, she assured him, she would miss him terribly. If all went well, he could expect her to return in the springtime. If, for any reason, she did not return, he must always remember that she had loved him dearly.

Packing only a few things and tucking the map deep in her pocket, Cara walked out the door of her childhood home and set off down the road. It was a beautiful clear morning, laced with birdsong. Gentle breezes nuzzled her hair, and she was surprised at the sense of optimism she felt. At eventide, she found a grassy spot by a stream. There she lay down for her first night alone. She covered herself with her warm woolen shawl and, exhausted, fell into a deep sleep.

In the morning, Cara awakened refreshed and energetic. The night sounds had not disturbed her at all! Her confidence soared. Perhaps this journey would be easier than she had thought! She gathered berries from the bushes, washed them in the clear stream and ate them with some of the bread she had brought for the trip. She thought about Broen, wondering how he had reacted to her leave taking.  She suspected that he would be sad and angry, yet somehow relieved by her seeking help.  Well, whatever his initial reaction, she knew he would be all right.  He had a full life with his work and the support of the townspeople.  He would ultimately benefit from her having taken these steps toward recovering her well being.  Once healed, she could return and resume their lives together.

The second day of travel was as delightful as the first.  The skies were clear and the breezes warm.  Even though the path was a little steeper and strewn with debris, she was making her way with remarkable strength.

Unfortunately, the third and fourth days proved much more difficult.  The soles of her shoes had worn thin from the pressure of the rocks.  Her feet and ankles ached.  The air was turning colder, and the wind grew harsh.  It was definitely more difficult to stay warm at night.  She had to search for enclosed places in the forest where she could build small fires to protect her from the cold.  The calls of the wild seemed louder and more menacing the farther she got from home.  Cara was aware for the first time how alone she was on this journey.  And on the evening of the fifth night, she wept from fear and exhaustion.

At dawn, she awakened to realize that she stood at the foot of the Great Mountain.  From here on, the path would be narrow and steep.  She studied the map and noted that the old woman had marked places where she might stop to rest.  She had even indicated the location of a cave where Cara might pass the night in safety.  For the first time,

Cara seriously considered turning back. This journey was proving to be more difficult than she had bargained for, and she was far from rested as she reviewed the prospects that were ahead. Her body ached, and her spirits were dimmed. Gone was the original optimism with which she had begun. She longed for the comfort and familiarity of her village. She stood on the path looking longingly in the direction of home. There was no sense in turning back now. She had already gone too far. With a deep and profound knowing that she had to continue, she turned and began her ascent up the mountain.

# Despair

The wind in the mountains was so fierce that Cara felt as if she were being beaten. Every step was an effort as she made her way slowly up the rugged pathway. The soles of her shoes had already worn through and, with each labored step, she felt the grinding roughness of the earth. It had been a full day since she had left the stream, and she needed to find some fresh water. But the trail was dry, almost parched. Worse still, her food was nearly gone. How would she make it if she didn't find food and water? She feared she had not planned well.

Cara made her way blindly now, placing one weary foot in front of another. In her exhaustion, she forgot why she had begun the journey in the first place. Now, surviving each step seemed to be the only motivation she had left. The map lay unopened in her pocket. As darkness enveloped her, she collapsed exhausted in a crevasse between two large rocks. No longer caring about the dangers that might accompany the sounds of the night, she slept.

That night, she dreamed of the crone. The old woman was sitting in a rocking chair in front of a large white farmhouse. Fields of bluebells surrounded the dwelling. The crone was waving to Cara, beckoning her forward. Cara couldn't hear what she was saying, as the ancient one was too far away, and her voice was erased by the howling wind. Cara tried to call out for help, but she could make no sound. She stumbled forward trying to hear the crone. No matter how many steps she took toward the farmhouse, she appeared to make no progress.

Cara awakened from the dream reminded of the crone and her map. How long had it been since she had consulted it? Where was it? Did she even know where she was? She rummaged through her things and found the folded piece of paper deep in her pocket. It was doubtful that a map would do her much good now. Even if she were on the right path, she was out of water and food, and her feet were too raw and blistered to carry on. Having nothing else to do, she sat huddled between the rocks and stared blankly at the crumpled paper.

Suddenly, she noticed something that had previously escaped her attention. The old woman had made some tiny drawings, almost too small to see. But as the morning sun rose in the sky and the light became brighter, Cara was able to see where she was. The old woman had drawn the very spot in which she was sitting. Below the crevasse, she had indicated a small blue pool, surrounded by areas of green.

"Silly old crone," Cara thought. "It is nearly winter. Even if I find this pool now, it is likely to be gone and doubtful that any green plants will remain. But I am thirsty, so it is worth trying." Cara struggled to stand on her swollen, bleeding feet and hobbled gingerly down the hillside in the direction of the pool. A pervasive chill had penetrated the mountains. The hillside was covered with a light dusting of snow. At that moment, Cara understood that the delay in beginning her journey might have cost her life.

Dark, menacing clouds raced across the sky. Another storm was coming, and this one would most certainly bring a heavier snow. Suddenly, Cara noticed an odd odor in the wind. Not unpleasant, really, but decidedly strange. As she continued down the hill, it became stronger. Yes, she knew that smell...sulfur. The old woman's map had indicated a hot sulfur spring! Excited by the prospect of warm healing liquid, Cara scrambled the rest of the way without noticing the pain in her feet.

Miraculously, the beautiful little blue pool was indeed a warm one, surrounded by green plants. Cara sat next to the water and gently removed her clothing. She pulled the tattered shoes from her swollen, mangled feet and gingerly immersed herself in the warm water. The sensation, at first painful, gradually relaxed her muscles and cleansed her wounds. As she sat in the water, she looked around. The pool was located in a small sheltered ravine. Giant trees surrounded the area, blocking the wind. Rocks had been piled near the steep cliff face, forming a fire pit. Others had obviously traveled here and used this as an oasis before. And what was this? To the left end of the cliff wall was an opening of some kind. Cara closed her eyes then, realizing that she could stay in the safety of this ravine until she had regained her strength. She laid her head back in the soft green plants and fell asleep.

# Respite

Cara was awakened by a burning sensation on her face. The searing blaze of the sun was directly above her. She had obviously slept in the warm water for several hours. Relaxed and comfortable for the first time in many days, she stretched her aching muscles in the warm pool. Feeling refreshed, she lay on the sunny bank for a few minutes until her skin had dried. She dressed and then examined her shoes. They were a definite problem. The holes in the soles were enormous. She could never finish her journey in these things!

Examining her feet, she was amazed at how much better they appeared. The water had cleansed her wounds. The blisters had softened and flattened and were far less tender.

Cara rummaged through her things to see if she could find something with which to mend her shoes. She found a piece of cloth in which she had wrapped her loaf of bread. Tearing the fabric in half and folding the pieces several times, she fashioned two crude, but smooth insoles. At least, the makeshift soles would provide some measure of insulation.

With the rest and the healing warmth, Cara's spirits had lifted some. However, she was still weak from hunger. She decided to explore the area to see if she could find something to eat. Suddenly, her mind's eye recalled the map, and she remembered the crone's drawings of green plants. "That's it," she thought. "The old woman wanted me to notice that there are edible plants here." Tasting a tender leaf, she confirmed that some of the greenery was watercress. The spring water, though warm and tasting of minerals, was fresh and quenched her thirst. She sat in the sheltered sunlight and ate her fill.

That afternoon Cara explored her surroundings further. Obviously, the cave in the hillside had been used for warmth and shelter by other travelers. Inside, someone had built a rock storage area in which there were nuts and dried berries. If worse came to worse, she could survive here for a time in this little oasis. She was filled with a lifting sensation, a feeling that was at once familiar and strange. Cara recognized the return of hope like the reconnection with a long lost friend.

She seriously assessed the situation. Snow was coming, at least here in the high mountains. It was too late to turn back toward home now. According to the map, she had come almost two-thirds of the way. If the crone was accurate, the summit was not far from here. Still, she could not climb the rest of the way on her damaged feet. The only option was to stay in the shelter and safety of the oasis until she was sufficiently rested and healed to continue.

And so Cara made a little home in the shelter of the ravine. During the day, she felt safe and warm, bathing in the springs and regaining her strength. How she dreaded the coming of the night. She suspected all sorts of animals would make their way to drink from the pool and feared they might bring her harm. As dusk fell, she retreated into the cave. It occurred to her to build a fire at the opening, a sort of protection between her and any dangers outside.

The first night was long and sleepless. With her back plastered against the cold wall of the cave, Cara trembled uncontrollably. Every sound brought terrifying images of fierce wild predators prepared to do her harm. Her heart echoed her fearful thoughts, flopping wildly against her chest cavity like a fish out of water, fighting desperately for breath in an unfamiliar environ.

However, that first long night passed without event, and dawn ushered in the promise of a new day. Obviously, her plan to place a fire between her and any unwanted guests had worked! She did see signs of animal tracks outside the cave, but they weren't very large. She felt somewhat reassured by her success, and the subsequent nights were less threatening.

By day, Cara ventured further and further from the safety of the little clearing. But, in the long dark hours of night, she was often filled with the dread of being so alone and vulnerable. Worse yet, she doubted her own judgment. She feared that she had made a terrible mistake leaving Broen. What on earth had she been thinking? Would he ever take her back? What were the villagers saying? They probably all thought she had gone mad. If she perished here in the mountains, would anyone ever know what had become of her?

"Perhaps I am mad," she muttered.

# The Final Effort

With the passage of days and nights, nightmares and solitude, Cara lost track of time. Light snowfalls came and went. Yet gradually, she healed. One morning, Cara awakened to a clear, sunny sky. The storm had passed, and the air felt significantly warmer. Intuitively, she knew the time had come to resume her journey. If she was going to make it over the summit, this was her chance. Slowly, she packed up her few belongings. She filled her pouch with water and stuffed her blouse with green plants and dried berries.

With great reverence, she cleared the little camp. Her eyes welled with tears as she uttered words of gratitude to the elements in the little oasis that had given her protection. Resolutely, she turned and made her way back up the hill to the path.

Back on the trail, Cara was disappointed to discover the cold, fierce wind that whipped across the mountainside. Though it was still sunny, the temperature on the ridge had dropped dramatically. Her hair slapped her face as if in a rage, and her eyes burned. The climb toward the peak was formidable. Fortunately, she had developed calluses on the bottom of her feet, and to her surprise, her legs actually felt strong.

When she finally reached the summit, she let out a cry of joy. The panorama was incredible! She could see the glen below stretching as far as the eye could see. The colors of fall were still bright across the landscape. Although she couldn't make out the Valley of the Bluebells, there was promise ahead. Her destination was within reach, and she knew she could make it.

The decent from the peak was gentle. This southern side of the mountain was greener and seemed much warmer. Toward evening, she found a stream and took cover under a large pine. "Perhaps tomorrow...," she thought as she drifted off to sleep.

The next day's journey took her further down the mountainside, but she still couldn't see her destination. It was the same the next day and the next. She was making her way off the mountain and certainly coming closer to the valley. Yet she seemed to make no real progress. "This is just like my dream," she thought. "I keep going and going, but I don't seem to get anywhere!"

When she finally reached the foothills, a dense fog had settled in. The pathway was visible barely a few yards ahead of her, so she made her way along carefully. Although it was gray, it did feel cozy, and she was relieved to be in the warmer temperatures. Suddenly, she noticed that the path no longer seemed to be open ahead. The fog was so dense that she couldn't see at all. A few steps further, and she was startled to realize that an enormous wall of cold gray rock obstructed the path.

On closer examination, Cara realized that this wall would be impossible to scale. It was steep and sheer. She followed along the wall to the right for an hour or so, and there was no break. Deciding the opening must be in the other direction, she retraced her steps and spent the rest of the day searching for a way to climb over. Darkness fell, and with it, her spirits. Cara was filled with rage. "Stupid, insane old crone! You brought me here with all sorts of promises. And after all my trials, it comes to this! How could you treat me with such cruelty? You are a monster, a monster!" Cara began to beat her hands wildly against the cold, unrelenting surface of the rock. Finally, with a mournful wail, she collapsed and lost consciousness at the base of the unforgiving gray barrier.

# The Valley

A soft breeze spun across her face. A downy coverlet spread over her body. "Oh," she thought, "I am dead. This is what it is like to be dead. A soothing, peaceful rest. Yes, that is it. I have died, and I am at peace." These thoughts were interrupted by the sharp pain in the soles of her feet and the ache coursing through the bones of her legs. "Oh, no, am I to take all my wounds into eternity?" she mused.

As Cara struggled to open her eyes and adjust her legs into a more comfortable position, she heard the sound of voices somewhere in the distance. The voices were lilting and soothing, almost like those of children. But no, they were not children's voices, they were women. Women's voices, laughing and chatting. Her eyes flew open, as she realized in the flash of a second that she was not dead. The pain in her legs, the breeze on her face and the sound of the voices all told her that. She looked about her and tried to sit up. A sharp pain clutched at her back, and she abandoned the effort. Instead, she turned her head from side to side taking stock of her surroundings.

She was in a tiny room. Her bed was no more than a narrow cot, but the pink coverlets that touched her body so gently smelled fresh and sweet. There was a pitcher of water on a small stand next to the bed. A tiny golden bell sat next to it, along with a vase of fragrant blue flowers. She looked the other direction and could see the treetops out the window. There was a bird's nest on one of the branches. She could hear, but not see, the chirping sounds of its inhabitants. I must be upstairs, she thought, but upstairs where? The effort of taking it all in became too much, and she allowed herself to once again sink into the soft downy pillows and into a deep sleep.

When Cara opened her eyes again, long gray shadows had fallen across the room. Somewhere, the women were singing. She tried to locate the origins of the sounds and realized they were outside. With a great effort, she thrust herself up into a half-sitting position, enough to allow her to look out the window onto the landscape below. What she saw took her breath away. There were fields and fields of blue flowers as far as the eye could see. Full green trees tinged with golden autumn dotted the landscape.

On the lawn just below her window, she could see a circle of women singing softly to the sound of a zither. It was difficult to make out their features from her angle of vision. One woman had long gray hair and sat on a chair. It was she who was playing the music. The others sat on the ground, brightly tinted skirts spread around them forming a rainbow of color.

At that moment, Cara realized where she was. She was in the Valley of the Bluebells! The woman playing the music must be the sister of whom the crone had spoken. She had succeeded! She had somehow completed her journey. Her eyes filled with tears, as she realized that all her pain and effort had brought her to her destination. Soothed by the gentle sounds of womansong, she wept silent tears of relief and gratitude.

Just then, the older woman cast her eyes heavenward. And as she did, she caught sight of Cara's face in the window. "Look Sisters," she cried aloud, "our guest has awakened! Welcome, my Dear! We are filled with joy to see your face!" The others cheered and began scrambling to their feet in excitement. Cara felt herself blush. She was both excited and embarrassed by this hearty welcome. After all, these people did not even know her. She had come to them injured, dirty and broken. And yet, their joy was so palpable, she could not help but smile. For in some strange way, her arrival appeared to be a cause for celebration for everyone.

The older woman spoke to one of the others. "Mira, please go to her and find out what she needs. We will continue our preparations here and will look forward to your reports."

"With joy!" responded Mira, a rotund woman with bright red hair and a sparkling smile. "I'll be up to tend to you, my Dear, just as soon as I draw and warm some bath water. There's a little bell beside your bed. Call me if you need me before I arrive." The circle of women broke into excited chatter as they dispersed.

Cara suddenly realized that she was exhausted from sitting up, even for such a short period of time. Her legs and back screamed in pain. Her mouth was parched. She let out a sigh and collapsed on the pillows as she awaited Mira's arrival. In a short while, there was a tap on the door and in bustled Mira. Her step was lively, despite her robust size, and her manner was both reassuring and compassionate. "Well, Dearie," she said. "We've wondered if you'd planned to sleep your life away. And how are you feeling now?"

Cara smiled weakly and tried to respond to Mira, but no sound came out at all. She let out a sigh that sounded like the moan of a wounded animal. She grimaced in pain as she tried to sit up.

"Not so good, Love?" replied Mira. "Well, don't worry. We'll have you better in no time. Lord knows you must have had a difficult journey. When we found you at the base of the hill, your hands and feet were in shreds, and you were barely breathing! You look a whole lot better now, I assure you. How about a warm bath? I have drawn the tub and filled it with scented rose petals. That will raise any lass' spirits, I'll wager. Can you walk if I help you? Here, lean on me."

Cara nodded and smiled back at Mira in gratitude. She liked this kind, happy woman. In fact, she reminded her of her Auntie. Just being in her presence was reassuring. Cara leaned heavily into Mira's side as she helped her up from the bed and supported her as she gingerly stood on her feet. Together the women made their way to the giant tub. It was in that moment that Cara knew her healing had begun.

# The Women

The first days in the Valley of the Blue-bells, Cara moved as if she were still in a fog. She would awaken, smile wanly at one woman or another, take nourishment and then fall again into a deep and often dreamless sleep. Her greatest compulsion was to rest. The sounds of the women going about their daily lives became background music for her healing slumber. Their chatter and songs, always in the distance, were soothing for this shattered soul.

Ever so gradually, Cara's strength returned. She still remained silent, unable to speak. The women seemed to understand. They didn't pressure her to tell them how she'd happened to come into their midst. They simply accepted her presence with the same calm with which they moved through their daily lives. These women seemed to dwell in the present, supporting one another and enjoying the beauty of the Valley.

As Cara recovered, she began to assist the others with their chores. She took walks in the fields with a tiny woman named Gaylan, gathering firewood or bouquets of blue blossoms for the evening table. By nature, Gaylan was a quiet young woman. Working side by side, the two shared a companionable, silent sisterhood.

In contrast, when she helped Mira in the kitchen, the air was alive with stories and ideas and the energy of preparing nutritious and beautiful meals. Mira entertained Cara with tales of herself as a girl and of her life as a mother of several children. At times, Cara wondered how a woman who had raised children had ended up in this place, obviously so far away from those she had loved. In her silence, she could not ask. And, frankly, it was a relief. She didn't want to pry or question. Her heart longed for the simplicity of accepting whatever Mira wanted to share and to have that be totally sufficient.

As the days went by, Cara noticed that she wasn't exactly homesick. Although she thought of Broen often, her life with him seemed far away and long ago. She still felt a profound love for her husband, as she did for her farm and the villagers. Yet, all of it was so distant, almost unreal. For the moment, there was no pain associated with the memories, no real longing. Just a cool smooth awareness that she held that life tenderly in her heart. It was startling for her to realize that she had walked away from her existence, had come to live among total strangers. Yet, she was at peace, at times even happy.

# *Restoration*

In the kitchen one day, Mira was weaving a tale so engaging that Cara let out a gurgling laugh. It was the first real sound she had uttered in so long! Both she and Mira stopped and stared at each other in stunned silence.

Mira finally broke their spellbound stillness. "Well, Dearie, it appears to me that you have some sort of voice still in you! That was a hearty laugh, I'll be tellin' you. And let's be clear. I'll wager if you let that one out, there will be more to follow. No hurry, mind you. But, Lass, you have been quiet for so long. Perhaps your heart is ready to speak again, eh?"

Cara stood facing Mira, who was at once serious and comical with her hands covered with flour and her apron splattered with dough. "Yes," she said in a quiet whisper. "Yes." Her voice sounded strange to her after such a long silence. It was weak, timid and hoarse. But she grinned nonetheless, because it was indeed the sound of her own voice. Mira wiped her floured hands on a towel and reached for Cara, drawing her into her ample bosom. "Oh Sweetie, Sweetie, you'll be just fine. No one here will pressure you to talk before you're ready. And when you do speak, your words will be heard with reverence and gratitude. These women here have seen and heard all of it - the joy and the pain. They know of life, and they are not afraid to hear it. You'll be all right. I'll wager, better than all right!"

The feel of Mira's arms around her moved Cara to a place of deepest longing. In that moment, she realized how much she had yearned to have a mother. How deeply she had craved the nurturing embrace of a woman who would hold her and guide her and offer her consolation and encouragement. In this moment, that is what Mira offered, the embrace of a loving mother. Leaning into the safety of Mira's embrace, Cara choked, as tears flowed down her cheeks blending with flour on her face. Mira held her solidly and did not move away. She understood that young Cara needed this moment desperately. The tears that flowed and the pain they carried would usher in a return to aliveness. Mira had seen this kind of profound grief before, and she was not afraid.

That evening in her bed, Cara tucked her head under the covers and tentatively tried out her voice. "Um," she croaked. "Ohhhh," she sighed. Both sounds came easily, so she tried others. "Oof," "Argk," and "Bah" all came out clearly. If she could make these sounds, she realized she would be able to talk again. Perhaps even sing....

Cara lay stone still in bed, her head tucked tightly under the covers. The awareness that she could talk filled her with a mixture of excitement and dread. She was excited, because if she could speak, she would reemerge and be able to participate more fully with the women. Right now, the feeling of dread was even stronger. She feared that her voice would bring out the stored-up pain, the fright and anger and despondency that had driven her from her home. What if she became that same defeated woman again? What if she would tell the same old story over and over and over again and nothing changed? What if the women found her story absurd and insisted that she return home to Broen and the wonderful life she had left behind? Would they judge her for having been so selfish in her leave taking?

Clearly, Cara wasn't ready to face any of these things. She certainly was not ready to contemplate going home. "No," she told herself silently, "I don't want to speak. I don't want all the judgments and expectations that come along with it." So Cara decided to remain silent a while longer in the hope that she could prevent the old, road-weary self from ruining the joy of her new home.

One day, Leah summoned Cara. "I have news from my sister," she said. "I know something of your village."

Cara sat silently. Life with the women had been so easy, so peaceful. Selfishly, she had not wanted to face the reality of home, the farm, the villagers and, most of all, Broen. Finally, she nodded.

"Well, I heard from my sister, who as you know dwells in the region from which you came. She said that there was some, um, difficulty...."

Alarmed, Cara forgot her decision to remain silent. "Oh, no! What?" she gasped. "Is it Broen? Is Broen all right?"

"Well, yes and no. It appears that right after you left, all went on as usual. Although terribly upset at first, Broen knew you needed help, and he accepted your decision. Of course, he also trusted that you would return. But after a while, the villagers began to miss the songs of your heart and your healing touch. The women wanted you there to attend their childbirths. Broen did everything he could to help them, giving them all the energy he had. Finally, the villagers became angry with him. They told him they wanted his methods to be more like yours. And they began to blame him for your having left.

"Broen continued on for a while, but he finally became exhausted. He complained of loneliness and missed your companionship. Then, try as he might, he seemed unable to fill all the demands that the villagers made of him.

Eventually, he gave away the animals and closed up the farm. Cara, Broen has left the village."

"He left? Left our home? The animals? What will the villagers do without him?" Cara stared at Leah in shock and disbelief, her thoughts racing. How could Broen leave? He had been so well respected, exactly what the villagers seemed to need. He was so strong! He appeared to have all the answers, everything he wanted from life. He was important to everyone! Missing me? He seemed not to need me for anything. Yet, she clearly understood what Broen must have gone through and how difficult it must have been for him to give up and leave the village. This awareness weighed heavily on her heart. She didn't speak any of her thoughts aloud. She smiled at Leah and replied ever so softly, "Thank you for telling me."

Leah looked at the face of her beloved Cara and realized that the young woman really had not comprehended how important she had been to her husband and to the villagers. True, Broen had many valuable qualities, much knowledge and physical prowess. But Cara had been a source of balance, bringing her open heart and healing touch to his life and work.

Leah held her own counsel. One day she would teach Cara that each person is unique and that all are necessary. In this case, both Cara and Broen had made a serious error in assuming that his way was better than hers. Leah patted Cara's cheek gently and merely said, "You are welcome. Try not to worry. This may have been for the best.

I am sure all will turn out well. I will want to talk with you more about this whenever you are ready. You may seek me out at any time."

# The Power of Stories

S pringtime was busy in the Valley of the Bluebells. The women planted. They cooked and
spun and raised animals. They did all the repairs of the large house and outbuildings. They
built large stone walls for the gardens. Each woman did
her part and each seemed to assume the chores best suited
to her natural skills. Some loved the more solitary tasks,
while others thrived on working with others.

As Cara recovered, she was able to move freely among them,
trying her hand at this and that. Having grown up with-

out a mother, there was much she did not understand about the ways of women. She was an eager apprentice, so the women enjoyed coaching her.

Although she could now speak, Cara's voice was still so soft it was difficult for the others to hear her. It was in the spinning room, where the women carded and spun the wool, that Cara became the most verbal. In the shelter of the cool, quiet room, the women taught her all about transforming the raw, rough piles of sheep's wool into soft strands of yarn. As they worked, they told one another the stories of their lives. These women spoke of girlhood and of the blossoming into women. They spoke of childbirth and the death of loved ones. The walls echoed the sounds of laughter and tears. Despite her youth, Cara soon found that she had her own stories to tell. The others were enthralled with her experiences and amazed by the wisdom of one so young.

As Cara's voice grew stronger, she began to tell her stories in more detail. She spoke of the loss of her mother and the profound connection she had felt with her father. She spoke of the unfolding of her healing gifts, how natural it had all been for her. Then, she explained how she had lost her confidence in the face of Broen's vast experience and knowledge, how his ways had seemed so superior to her own.

Finally, she spoke of becoming weakened and ill, even though she had a very comfortable existence as Broen's wife. She told of the isolation and desperation that had driven her to confide in the strange old crone and how that had led to the painful decision to leave home in search of help. And she spoke of her guilt because she had left Broen behind.

At times, Cara would be overcome with emotion as she recounted her history. The women held her whenever her tears flowed. They supported her as she searched her memory for bits of clarity and insight. Mostly, she felt loved and accepted.

However, there were times when one or another of the women would challenge her thinking or disagree with her perceptions. At first, Cara was startled. She had hoped to avoid conflict in the Valley; but here it was, directed toward her! Whenever this happened, her throat would tighten, and she would shrink back in silence, just as she had before leaving the village. She was terribly uncomfortable and regretted having been willing to reveal her story. This was exactly what she had feared would happen!

As time went on, she became more accustomed to being questioned. Usually, it was done in a supportive manner, and Cara realized it helped her see things from a different perspective. Sometimes, after reflecting on what had been said, she could accept that she had been blind to some aspect of her personality or her situation. Gradually, she learned to admit to her shortcomings and to take responsibility for her actions.

She also recognized that some of the input she received was too harsh or inaccurate. In this case, it was difficult for her to stand up for herself and to disagree with another's strong opinion. She studied other women as they worked through their disputes and learned that it could be done firmly, without doing harm. Her first attempts at debate were awkward and tentative, coming out as little more than feeble croaks. But each time she succeeded in speaking honestly, she stood up a bit taller and developed the courage of her convictions.

Recounting her story, particularly the part about the old crone and the map, brought about some confusion and anger within Cara. It was only by sheer luck that the women had discovered her ravaged body at the base of the stone wall. In fact, she would have died had she lain there much longer! Clearly, the crazy old crone had led her astray. She dwelled on this betrayal over and over again, wondering why the old woman would have brought her that close to her destination without telling her that her way would be blocked as she neared the Valley.

Finally, she grew tired of thinking about it and wanted to find some peace. She sought out Leah for help. As always, Leah was warm and calm, listening as Cara made her complaints about her elderly sister. Cara finished by saying, "I am not able to forgive her, Leah. I came close to dying, and it was almost as if she led me intentionally to that point. I just don't understand."

Leah responded in a calm, clear voice. "I don't want to defend my sister. I am curious about the map she gave you. Do you still have it?"

"I don't know," answered Cara impatiently. It had been so long since she had seen it; she imagined it had been lost along the way. "I suppose I can look in my room among my things. But if you think she had indicated the wall, I am sure she did not! I recall her showing a direct pathway from the base of the mountains to the Valley of the Blue-bells."

Later, Cara frantically searched among the objects that remained from her journey - a few dried berries, some crumpled greens, a shiny stone from the path. Among these things, she discovered the shredded piece of paper. It was faded, nearly illegible, but she could still make out some of the pale markings. Eager to prove her point about the crone's carelessness, she grabbed the map and took it to Leah.

Leah smiled as she recognized her sister's handwriting on the tattered piece of paper. "Well, it's a good thing my sister is not a map maker, huh? Perhaps you can teach me about the various signs that she indicated along your journey." Cara did so, noting the paths, crevasses, mineral pool and cave. Wanting to prove her point, her eyes moved quickly to the portion of the map where the stone precipice would have been. She was astonished, and not a little embarrassed, to see that it had been drawn there quite clearly. In fact, there had also been an indication of an entryway on one end of the wall. The crone had marked this narrow passage way with the words "Pilgrim's Pass."

Cara gasped, staring at Leah in shame. "I feel so foolish. How mean-spirited of me to have blamed your sister for my misfortune. Actually, I caused my own downfall. In my exhaustion and fury, I failed to consult the map. Forgive me, Leah, for this hasty and unfair accusation!"

Leah smiled. "I am truly quite pleased that you came to me with your fury, Cara. All of us have blind sides, especially when we are exhausted or angry. When you arrived at the gray stone wall, your journey had been hard. For many miles, a dense fog had obscured your way. It is quite understandable why you forgot the map.

"I do believe there is an important lesson here. Sometimes, we think we know exactly where we are going, and we just charge forward blindly. In our own haste and preoccupation with the destination, we fail to pause and ask for guidance along the way. It is always important to revisit our guidance periodically, so that we can take it into consideration given our current state of affairs. That is the meaning of the map." One more time, Leah had provided Cara with an important life lesson.

# The Fullness of Self

*L*eah and the other women seemed available to Cara for whatever she needed. In this nurturing environment, she began to heal at ever deeper levels. It showed first in her eyes. The dark circles faded. Then her cheeks regained their color. Her body filled out, straightened up. Her steps were sure as she walked among the bluebells. Her voice returned, until she was blessed with full volume and resounding laughter.

No one was ever able to exactly recall when Cara began to sing again, but they all agreed that it happened around the time that she began to take care of the animals. You see, as she grew stronger, she made her way to the pens more frequently. The sight of the goats and chicks and rabbits made her heart soar! At her core, Cara felt united with these wonderful creatures. Her first day in the pens, she gingerly lifted a small bunny, nuzzling his fur. Something about the feel of his tiny heart beating against her palm brought back a part of Cara that had been long forgotten. She ached to reconnect with the little girl she had once been.

Little by little, she took over the duties of caring for the animals. She milked the goats and fed the smaller animals, delighting in the sights and sounds and smells that surrounded her. She was particularly fond of Nana, the oldest of the female goats. The two became close companions, as Nana always accompanied Cara while she did her chores. Cara was also the first to note that Nana was pregnant. This was the cause of some alarm among the women, because Nana had nearly died the previous season when she had given birth. So Cara watched over the mother goat with great care.

When Nana's kids were born, Cara was there. As expected, the delivery was difficult, and her midwifery skills were useful. The women gathered silently at the side of the pen, marveling at the ease with which Cara dealt with the situation. She expertly delivered the twins and did all she could to help Nana. Cara stroked Nana's face and placed the kids near their mother to nurse. All was in vain. Nana took her last breath, her nose nuzzled in Cara's palm while her babies nursed.

One by one, the women moved silently away from the tender scene, leaving Cara alone with her lost Nana Goat and the newborns. She sobbed as she bade her dear friend farewell, vowing to care for the kids.

As promised, Cara fostered and pampered the babies, and they thrived in her care. She named the twins Alpha and Omega. The women could not help but smile as they watched Cara's love pour onto her new little charges. The tiny goats scampered at her heels, following her everywhere. And Cara was, once more, at home in her being.

Life among the women held beautiful rewards for Cara. She came to know each of them quite well, learning about the lives they had prior to coming to the Valley. Among them were mothers, daughters and sisters...lovers, wives and friends. Each had come to the Valley for her own particular reasons. Each had unique gifts, as well. Like Cara, many reported they had known about their special abilities, even practiced them, prior to coming to this place. Others had only begun to explore life's meaning and purpose since coming to join the women. Their greatest commonality was that they all believed that they had a great purpose to serve and wanted to find a way of doing so. The home in the Valley provided safety and support for that quest. In this company, Cara felt less ashamed of her quirks and learned to appreciate her own uniqueness as the product of her soul's expression.

To her surprise, Cara began to feel restless. Even though she was content, her mind tended to wander from her tasks. She would fantasize about her village, or wonder about the state of the farm. She thought about Broen and about their relationship. Despite their lack of connection, she realized she still loved him. Many questions were now unanswered. Would it ever be possible for them to find one another and reconnect? She had changed significantly, she knew. Would that make things between them better or even worse? Would there be room for her expanded sense of self in their marriage? She now understood that while they were so different, both she and Broen had valuable skills to offer. She longed to tell him so. Yet, she wondered if he would ever trust her again.

At other times, Cara's mind drifted toward entirely new themes. She imagined places she'd never been, oceans and forests. She thought of children and elders that she might nurture in far-off lands. She recalled her apprenticeship with the midwife and how much she had enjoyed being a student. Perhaps there was a way she could continue to study. She realized that there was much life still to be discovered, a fact that both excited and frightened her.

One day, she approached Leah. "Do all the women come here and stay?"

"Oh, my, no!" exclaimed Leah. "Some have made that decision, of course. There are ten of us who have decided, for whatever reason, that this Valley is our permanent home. Our peace lies in remaining here and offering our gifts of service to those who come. Many women arrive, as you did, having lost their voices and seeking refuge or respite. Others come on a specific spiritual quest. Many reasons, really. But most women decide to move back into the world in some way.

"Take for example Vive. She left us just before you arrived. While here, Vive made the decision that she wanted to marry and raise children. Masa has decided to go back and make a home for the elderly in her village. Dees, the one that entertains us with her harp? She has realized that her life's purpose is to teach music to poor children. Undine feels called to live near the ocean. Beyond that, she is not sure what she will do. Is it not marvelous how each of us is so alike, yet so very different?"

There was a pause. "And, you, Cara? What is happening for you?"

Cara was confused. "I have been so very happy here. I feel as though I belong, as if you and the others are my family," she replied. "I was desperate and forlorn when I came. Now that I am feeling stronger, I am recovering parts of myself that I had lost. I feel more alive, filled with energy. My voice is vibrant, and I am able to croon again. My inner life seems clearer. I am able to stand tall in the face of disagreement. You and the others have filled so many unmet needs for me; you have been mothers, sisters, teachers and friends. I dread the thought of leaving! Yet, there is a part of me that believes I am to do just that."

Leah listened without interruption. Finally, she said, "Cara, you will know when it is time, and you will know what you are to do. A quiet, but clear prompting of your heart will simply say, 'now' and 'yes.' Wait for your heart's calling. Until then, you can remain with us."

Cara waited, and she peacefully passed another winter with the women in the Valley.

# The Circle

Cara watched with awe as the snows began to disappear from the distant mountains. Tiny green plants burst forth expectantly throughout the Valley. And with their appearance came Cara's realization that it was time to leave. Her own soul was also fertile, ready for new growth.

Although Cara told no one, Leah sensed the shift that had taken place. One day, the wise one approached her. "I want to speak to you if I might," Leah began. Cara nodded, so she continued. "I have watched you heal and re-gain your strength. Clearly you are looking quite robust. And, of course, your connection with the animals has re-kindled your healing powers. However, I believe that there is one more piece to be done before you are ready to take your leave."

Cara was silent. By now, she trusted Leah completely. There was, indeed, still a part of her that felt somehow raw and incomplete, though she could not name it. Cer-tainly, she had no idea what Leah would suggest.

"We often have a ceremony here, a type of initiation be-fore a woman leaves our midst. In this ceremony, we pro-vide the woman with the opportunity to make peace with her life, all that has gone before and what is to come. With your consent, I want to set a time in the near future for us to have such a ceremony for you." Cara agreed, and the time was set.

When the day arrived, she was instructed to relax and spend time alone in quiet contemplation. In this way, she would prepare herself for what was to come. With some diffi-culty, Cara followed these instructions. It felt odd to be excluded from the preparations for this community event. It was a delightful day, filled with birdsong and gentle breezes. The bluebells shone in their glory, mirroring sis-ter sky in their color and magnificence.

The women were obviously excited, each purposeful in her own particular task. By afternoon, the preparations were complete, and the women disappeared suddenly leaving Cara alone in the garden. This was the place where she had first seen the women from her upstairs bedroom. She grimaced at the memory of how beaten and broken she had been when she arrived.

Now, she was overcome with the beauty of her surroundings. Everything had been decorated, with garlands of wild flowers and ribbons adorning the already magnificent scene. Tables had been set up for the feast that would follow the ceremony. There was the zither, and a few other hand-held instruments, so obviously they planned music and dancing. Cara was overcome by the blessing of it all. Even more, she felt astonished that so much had been done in her honor.

When all was in readiness, the women filed in one by one and took their places in a circle. Cara decided to sit facing the tree and the window of her little bedroom above.

Leah began the ceremony. "Sisters," she began, "Cara has been a treasure among us. In your own way, each of you has contributed to the brightness that she now embodies. Soon, she will leave us. This afternoon, it is our final task to offer her the wisdom and support that will allow her to fully embody all that she is. We will honor the woman in Cara, as maiden, as mother and as crone. I am going to ask Gaylan to begin."

Gaylan, usually so quiet and shy, stood and began to speak. Her cap of black curls glistened in the afternoon light. "I speak for the maiden," she said. Cara thought how fitting that this pixie of a woman would speak on behalf of the child. "The maiden is the young one in all of us. She is the bright little star that enters the world filled with promise. In her is the seed of every woman's destiny. The maiden is also the growing girl; she who faces what life brings and finds ways to survive in the face of its trials. The maiden is the teenager who leaves the child's body behind, the dawning of womanhood."

Gaylan sat down, and Leah spoke. "Cara," she said, "tell us of yourself as the maiden. It was not so long ago, so surely you can recall. What were your gains and what were your losses? Give us the gift of your stories."

Cara stood. "I was a happy child, drawn by my heart to all the living creatures around me. I was blessed by a father who exuded gratitude for my being. I was raised by a kindly neighbor woman as the youngest among her brood. I was well loved. I was encouraged to become what I was born to become. I always knew I was born to be a healer. Those were my gifts.

"But there were losses, too, and grave times. My mother was not able to care for me. She left when I was a mere babe in arms, never to visit me again. I always felt the emptiness of her absence. Although there were wonderful women in my life who treated me with great care and kindness, I never knew a mother's love. Not until," she paused, choking on her words and looking at Mira's glowing countenance, "not until I came here and felt Mira's warm welcoming embrace.

"There were other losses, too. I felt very different because of my healing gifts. I never really felt like I fit in. It was only my father, Colin the farmer, who made me feel truly accepted. When he died, I was just entering the fullness of young womanhood. And so, I entered that time, alone and isolated."

"And what did you learn from all of this, Cara?" Leah asked gently.

Cara thought a moment and responded. "I learned to be independent, to take care of my own needs. I learned that there was value in expressing the gifts with which I was born. I learned that not everyone will like or understand me...or even love me. But I learned to give and receive kindness where it was truly offered. And I learned that despite the depth of grief and loss, there is a spirit within me that is always capable of healing."

Leah bowed in Cara's direction. She then invited any of the women who wanted to speak to do so, sharing about their own experiences as maidens.

When this was finished, Leah asked Mira to rise and address the group. "Mira, all of us know you as a wise mother. Please speak to us of a woman as mother."

Mira struggled to lift her girth from the ground. She had aged considerably since Cara first arrived, and Cara felt a pang of fear to notice that the woman's vibrant red hair was now heavily laced with gray. Once on her feet, Mira spoke with as much authority and conviction as ever.

"The stage of mother is a powerful one for women. This is the time when the woman learns to function as an adult. During this time, many marry and bear children. Others will give birth in other ways, becoming artists, teachers and healers. Women in this stage are meant to hone their skills, build their strengths and express their gifts to the world. Unfortunately, they often find themselves with too many demands and can get distracted. Some women doubt themselves when they are told they are not worthy to express opinions. During this time, many become silent, even turning away from their natural gifts. They live to care for others, which in itself is a wonderful gift. Unfortunately, many forget who they are during this time and become hopelessly lost to themselves."

Leah spoke again. "Cara, you are right now in the stage of mother. You have born many gifts in this world already. Speak to us of yourself as mother. What have been the gains and the losses so far?"

Again, Cara contemplated the enormity of the question. She began. "As I said, my father died at the time I left my girlhood. So my entry into this stage of life was confused, often unstable. I recall, though, that there was a poignant event in which a mother and her daughter came to visit me. The child had once been in my care, and they came to help me at the time when I had no will to live. Now that I think about it, the woman Adele was quite good at mothering me. It was under her nurturing care that I recovered from my grief. So, I guess I could say that I entered womanhood in a state of despair, yet found renewed hope in the care of a mother and her child.

"So far, I have had many opportunities to give birth to my gifts. In my village, I was respected and valued as a healer. I had wonderful training from a midwife. And though I have never given birth to my own children, I have certainly been present when many newborns came into the world. These have been the gains thusfar."

She paused, wondering how she could speak of her marriage to Broen. "Many of you know I also married as a young woman. There were both gains and losses in this relationship. I learned much from Broen about healing and about living with another person and about letting go of my need to be the center of attention. But somewhere along the line, as Mira said, I lost myself. Without realizing it, I gradually lost my sense of substance and became little more than a hollow shell. Then, I literally lost my voice. That is when I came to you. So, you can see there have been many gains and many losses so far.

"I must also say that I have learned from each of these things. During my time with you, I have come to understand that what I bring to the world and what Broen brings to the world, though very dissimilar, are equally important. I have come to value the knowledge I gained from him and understand the need to integrate it with my own heartfelt inclinations. I hope that, one day, I will be able to speak to him of these things. For, despite the pain I endured, I am more whole from having gone through the trials of the past few years."

The women were silent, inspired by Cara's wisdom. In turn, several spoke of their own lives in the stage of mother. Having listened to Cara, they were reminded that life's trials can be fruitful if allowed to be so. Thus, when the women spoke, there was a power in their own reflections.

Finally, Leah said, "I, as the oldest among you, will speak as crone. Most of you will not reach this stage for many years. And, yet, my wish for all of you is that you come to know the fullness of this stage of life. Being a crone has often held a negative connotation, being confused with ugliness and loss of vigor. I stand before you to call that idea into question.

"The crone has an important role to play in the world. It is she who dares to integrate all of life's parts, the physical, mental, emotional and spiritual. The crone has lived long enough to have garnered wisdom over the years. Now, I caution you, do not assume this insight is inevitable with the coming of age. Many women refuse to change, to grow, and to continually expand their base of wisdom. These grow old as grizzled, bitter beings. So, to truly become a wise woman, you will need to be willing to bend, even break, in order to learn all life has to offer.

"As the crone, the wise woman if you will, I have the opportunity to lay aside some of the struggles of the earlier stages. Women in my stage of life are no longer raising young children, so they have the ability to raise up the world. It is their responsibility to speak the truth as they see it, even when it is not popular. It is because I am older that I can explore life without harsh judgment, but with great discernment. Do not dread this time, Dear Women. Hear me that while aging has its losses of youthful vigor and its share of aches and pains, it is the richest of the stages.

"Cara, it will be many years before you will become a crone. Though, I must say, I wish I could be alive to see you when that time arrives! Who knows what life experiences still await you? I am certain that you will meet each of them as you have met your life so far: with courage, with stamina, with integrity and with great love. Have you anything to share about becoming a wise woman?"

Cara thought a moment, and then she stood facing the women. "It was a wise crone who found me in my despair and guided me to this place of healing. It is due to her discernment and her willingness to make an unpopular recommendation that I was able to continue to live. I owe my very life to this woman's wisdom."

Then, tears in her eyes, Cara looked around the circle of women. Her heart overflowed with gratitude. One by one, she spoke to each of the inspiration they had given her during her stay. At one time or another, each had been a teacher; each had met a need within her.

When she had finished, Leah stood. "The women have a gift for you," she said. Mira came forward bearing a woven cape of such beauty and softness that it took Cara's breath away. Mira placed it around her shoulders, saying, "Lass, this has been woven especially for you from the yarn made during your stay. Its threads hold the memories of our stories, the spirit of our time together. Wherever you go, wherever you are, you will always be in our hearts. When you feel lonely and need the loving touch of another, wrap yourself in this garment and call us forth in your heart. We will never fail you in our love."

As dusk crept across the Valley, the bluebells turned a deep purple and the crimson clouds faded into the night sky. Cara stood, her cape draped across her shoulders, and she sang. Her voice, full and vibrant, blanketed the landscape and embraced all the creatures with her lovely healing songs.

With that, Leah declared the ceremony complete, and the festival began. The women ate and laughed; they played music and danced. The celebration lasted long into the night.

# The Return

ara's last morning with the women was calm, almost uneventful. She made her final preparations for the journey back across the mountains. As she cleared away her things, her mind reviewed her time among the women. Despite her sorrow, she knew that it was time to leave them and set forth on her journey home.

Everyone was attentive, making sure they said their goodbyes, each dealing with the departure in her own

unique style. Some gave Cara small tokens, others carefully prepared food for the journey. When it came time to
leave they formed a small procession as they ushered her
through the fields of bluebells toward the gray wall. Alpha and Omega were to accompany her, so everyone was
reassured that her trip would not be as lonely as before.

Instead of struggling up and over the rock wall, Leah took
Cara's hand and led her through the Pilgrim's Pass. It was
at that juncture that she said her last goodbye to the wise
woman who had been her mentor. "How can I express
the depth of my gratitude, Leah, for who you are and what
you do? How can I tell you what my time with you has
meant? I don't know how I could ever begin to repay your
kindness."

Leah took Cara's hands in hers and looked directly into
her eyes. "Repay me," she said earnestly, "by becoming
the woman you were always meant to be. Repay me by
becoming a wise woman until the end of your days. That
is your destiny." With those last simple words, Leah turned
and walked back into the Valley with the others, back to
the work that was her own destiny.

Cara's return from the Valley was less fearful and challeng-
ing than her original pilgrimage. Draped in her shawl,
with Alpha and Omega dancing at her heels, she made
her way up the path. At one high point, she turned and
could still catch sight of the house and the meadow below.
The women were still there, lined up along the path, watching her as she made her gradual ascent up the hillside.

Not sure whether they could see her, she called to them and waved one last goodbye. Suddenly, the landscape was enveloped by the same dense gray fog that had been there when she first arrived. The Valley and the women disappeared in an instant, and Cara felt the anguished pull of separation.

"Well," she said to the young goats. "It's just the three of us now. Let's go. I think I can recall a place that would be comfortable for the night and have some water and grass for you. And of course, I won't forget to consult my map this time!" The little goats responded to the enthusiasm in her voice and matched it by romping gaily ahead.

And so the journey went. Though the trail was as arduous as it had been before, Cara was in much better shape. She felt strong, and she moved with steadfast determination. The summer breezes were gentle, and the way was clear.

By day, she made steady progress, admiring the beauty of the lush green mountains. At night, she lay beneath the stars, recalling the moments with her beloved companions. Curled up with her kids and sheltered by the shawl the women had given her, she would allow herself to fall into serene sleep.

Cara was both surprised and reassured at the ease with which she made her way back across the mountain. She had not realized she had grown so strong, both physically and mentally. This return journey was not always easy, and more than once, she lost her way. A wiser woman now, she would calmly consult her map and was always able to put herself back on track. Cara felt a profound confidence in her ability to face whatever challenges came her way.

Along the path were familiar landmarks, each a reminder of her other grueling journey. The most poignant moment came when she reached the crevasse and smelled the sulfur wafting from the canyon below. The smell brought memories of the healing respite she had spent there. She made a decision to pass some time in the ravine, enjoying the hot water and sleeping again in the cave.

As she left the path and made her way down the hill, she was delighted to see that the clearing looked quite different than when she last had visited. It was generously adorned with the vibrant greens of spring. Tiny flowers swayed in the breezes and seemed to turn their colorful faces in order to get a better view of the young woman who was entering their midst. The old trees recognized Cara at once and waved their bright green foliage in welcome.

The spot also delighted Alpha and Omega. They immediately set off in search of fresh things to eat. Cara sat at the edge of the pool, mesmerized by the beauty of the little oasis. There were no signs of anyone having been in the clearing or the cave since she had last passed this way. The rock storage area was empty. Cara smiled as she remembered that she still had more than enough dried fruit and nuts in her pack and would be able to replenish the supply.

As before, Cara built a small fire outside the mouth of the cave. It brought warmth and light to the clearing. She felt safe in the company of her two young kids, as they jostled for the most comfortable spot inside the cave. That night, she dreamed of the crone. The old woman was in Cara's garden at home. As the younger woman drew closer to the scene, she could hear that the crone was crooning softly to herself. And she was not alone. Perched atop her shoulder was the same little sparrow that had died in Cara's palms! Far from dead, he warbled with all his might. Cara listened to their shared melody and, though there were no real words, the melodic message was clear. They sang:

> *Cara comes home, our Cara comes home.*
> *Child of this land, our Cara comes home.*
> *Cara comes home, our Cara comes home.*
> *Strong and secure, she makes her way home.*
> *Gift to the world, our Cara comes home.*

Cara and the goats passed three happy days and nights in the clearing before she felt ready to leave. On the last morning, she made sure that all was just as she had found it, except that the cache for the food had been refilled and the stones carefully replaced. As one last gesture of love, she sprinkled the seeds of bluebells that she had brought with her from the Valley.

"You will just love these little blue friends I have brought you!" she confided to the flowers. "They smell wonderful and will give you company well into the fall. I leave them with you. May they be a reminder to all weary travelers that there is always hope and help ahead."

# The Choice

**B**efore she expected it, Cara had traversed the Great Mountain and found herself at a crossroad. Puzzled, she consulted her new map and saw that indeed this junction was indicated. She had not noticed this spot before, as the pathway from her village had merged directly with the path over the mountain. Now she realized she had several choices. If she proceeded straight ahead, the trail would take her directly back to the village of her birth. Studying the map more closely, she noted that the fork to the right ultimately lead to the sea. And to the left, there was a vast forest, through which she must pass in order to arrive at an important city.

Cara was surprised to find herself considering her options. Wasn't she going "home"? She had always assumed that meant returning to her farm, taking up her healing work and living out her years there. Now it occurred to her that she had more choices than she had ever before contemplated. She also felt the need to find Broen. Perhaps she could offer him help. Or at least let him know that she understood the role they had each played in their parting.

It was late in the day, so Cara decided to make her camp at this crossroads and spend some time contemplating her predicament. For the first time in a long time, Cara felt confused and frightened. "I thought I was going home," she mused aloud. "Home. I thought this journey was about returning. But what is home? Where is home? Is it a place? The house in the village? The marriage? The Valley of the Bluebells? I am not sure anymore what home means to me. How can I possibly go there if I don't know where it is? I no longer know how to make such a choice. Only a few days out of the comfort of the Valley, and I am already in a terrible quandary!"

Just then, Cara became aware of a presence, sensing that someone or some thing was watching her. The goats seemed relaxed enough, showing no signs of any disturbance. Suddenly, directly in front of her stood the old crone.

"Aha,' the woman said with a chuckle. "It is the young Cara making her return from my sister's Valley! And how did you find it? Did your body and soul mend?"

Cara looked at the gnarled hands that clutched the top of the cane. How had she failed to see the incredible beauty in these experienced, life-worn hands? "Thanks to you, yes. I am very well. During my time there, I learned so much. Though it was not always easy, I was well loved and supported. My soul was filled in places that I never knew were empty. And, as you can see, I have regained my voice and am ready to make my way back into the world. I owe you so much for seeing my need and urging me to go. I owe you my very life. I am deeply grateful!"

"Good!" said the crone abruptly. "Granted, I pointed the way. But you must always remember that it was your spirit that led you to the Valley. It was your own willingness to be healed that allowed the transformation to occur. Now Girl, what is next? I hear you moaning and groaning about another life dilemma. Have you not had enough pain for a while?"

"Well, suddenly I realize that I have more choices than ever! I find myself at this crossroads wondering which way to go. I have spent long hours weighing the potential gains and losses of each pathway. If I go straight ahead, I will arrive at the village of my birth. I have longed for the familiarity and safety of the people and the farm. Yet, the path to the left also shows great promise. It eventually leads to a large city. One of the women in the Valley told me of this place. There, I could pursue my studies and satisfy my love of learning. The path to the right leads to the sea. I know the least about this choice. Yet, something within me would like to spend time there. They tell me the shore can be a source of great peace and inspiration.

"So you see, there are things I appreciate about each of these choices. There are also ways that I fear them all. The situation feels quite uncertain and overwhelming.

"And, of course, there is Broen. I desperately want to find him, but I have no idea where to look. If I knew where he was, I could begin there.

"Further, I realize I no longer am certain what it means to go home. I am quite afraid that I will make a wrong choice and unknowingly send myself in a misguided direction. What if I make a bad decision?"

"Ah," said the old woman softly. "That's the joy of it, you see. Each of these paths holds a somewhat different future. Each will have its own twists and turns, different people, different scenery. Even more, there will be blessings and challenges associated with each of them. None of these will be revealed to you at this juncture, but you can be assured that they are there.

"Don't frighten yourself by believing that there is only one choice. Perhaps each path has its rewards. Knowing you, you will be able to navigate your way through any of them, and quite handily, I might add. Remember, you are coming to this moment in time with all the strength and knowledge and courage you have gleaned from your life so far.

"True, to favor one path over the others will mean that there are two you did not choose. Something will be lost, certainly. And something will be gained. That is far too scary if you believe you must choose the path with no losses and only gains. But what if you viewed this from another angle? What if you sat in silence and asked your heart which path is most peaceful to choose at this time? You can always change your mind in the future and move in another direction."

Cara reflected on this and asked, "What if I am wrong? I am afraid of making a mistake! I would rather trust your experience to help me make this decision. You were right before. Won't you just tell me which way you think I should go?"

The crone smiled kindly. "What is being wrong anyway? Does being wrong mean there will be trials, hardships, pain? That's a given in life, no matter which way you proceed. Does being wrong mean that you are forever prisoner to this choice? No, you can always alter your situation, making changes as you go. Does being wrong mean you will disappoint someone? Who might you disappoint? Those who truly love you want one thing above all else...that you live in peace and joy. To do that, you must seek your answers out of love, not out of fear. How can you possibly lose your way when your direction is toward peace?

"No, Cara, I cannot make this choice for you. I can see that you have given each of your choices great thought. Now you must balance your thinking with your heart's desire. You must go to your own heart to seek your final answer. There, and only there, will you find your direction home.

"I am certain that you and Broen will meet again, because you both have things that must be said, feelings that must be understood. You now recognize that the world needs you both. He, too, has been on a difficult journey and will likely have learned a great many new lessons himself. Who knows what will happen when the two of you are reunited? That will be revealed as you move along your paths. I offer one caution, Cara. Do not make his life your whole journey. Otherwise, you will find yourself lost once more. And that serves neither of you. Rather, join him in the fullness of who you are and do so as a part of your heart's desire."

Cara had so many questions, but before she could respond, the crone waved her hand and was gone. Again, she was amazed by the quickness with which the old woman moved.

Deep within her, Cara knew that the woman was speaking from a place of profound wisdom. Still young, she could only grasp part of the crone's message. She had wanted more answers, wanted to find out exactly how things were going to work out for her. At the same time, she felt reassured and trusted that with the morning light, she would know what to do next.

As the sun rose over the horizon, Cara awakened and rose to her feet. She opened her arms as if to embrace the day and breathed in the clarity of the crisp morning air. Turning toward the path she'd just traveled, she said her thanks for all that had gone before. She surveyed the crossroads at which she found herself. Placing her hand on her heart, she silently blessed the entry to each of the trails that extended from the cross in the road. A beam of light illuminated the pathway of her choice. She smiled broadly as she wrapped herself in her woven cape. Sensing they were about to go, Alpha and Omega scrambled impatiently at her heels.

Then, with great strength and determination, Cara planted her feet firmly on the earth and moved in the direction of her dreams.

# Acknowledgments

*T*hroughout the development of this project, I have been blessed by the support and assistance of a number of remarkable people. I trust them, and they each made a unique contribution.

Thank you from the bottom of my heart to the three muses who meet with me every month and remind me of the importance of mentoring, creativity and mutual support: Mary Lou Cook, Mary Ann Shaening and Courtney Cook. This piece of work would not have been completed without your help and inspiration.

Special credit is due my trusted colleague, Linda Todd, who helped me balance the creativity of myth with sound psychological theory and professional experience, and always with patience and good humor.

Several people made valuable suggestions for the manuscript itself: Linda Barr, Lisa Buckley, Mary Ann Liebert, Deborah Maddox, Katie Montgomery, Louise Pietrafesa and Blythe Richfield. I appreciate Nancy Goldberger for having posed the difficult questions.

I want to recognize Jill Kahn, my friend and colleague, who has taught me about the importance of ritual. The celebration in the book is modeled after her fine work.

Thank you to Maggie O'Reilly for her editorial skills and keen insights.

I also wish to express my appreciation for the professional mentoring I receive from two extraordinary wise women, Lee Davis, Ph.D. and Marilyn Matthews, M.D. Your work is exemplary, always an inspiration to me.

I am deeply grateful to my husband and friend, Bernardo, who supported me throughout. Thank you for believing in me yet again.

Finally, I want to acknowledge the women I have been privileged to serve over the years, both as an educator and therapist. Each of you has been a teacher for me, reminding me of the myriad of ways a woman can walk this earth.

*~Catherine Monserrat~*

*Reading Group Questions and Topics for Discussion*

1.  The tale begins with a love story, but Colin and Selene have an unfortunate ending to their relationship. What were the warning signs that they refused to see? At first glance, it appears that Selene was to blame for the problems in the marriage. In what ways was Colin also responsible?

2.  As a young girl, Cara begins to show a propensity for healing. What were the blessings and the disadvantages of her childhood situation? Do you think most children are born with inherent gifts?

3.  What is the symbolism of the child, Anna Cara, in relationship to Cara's grieving process? Why was she able to reach Cara when no one else could?

4.  Everyone in the village develops very high expectations of the young scholar, even before he arrives. How do you explain this intense reaction to a stranger?

5.  Cara decides to imitate Broen's work. Why would she do this when she had been successful with her own?

6.  What does the crone represent? How do you explain her statement, "...I fear the loss of your voice is a symptom of something far more serious"?

7.  At the warning of a total stranger, Cara decides to separate from Broen and make a journey on her own. This is certainly impulsive, and perhaps very dangerous. Why would Cara listen to the old woman? What do you see as the real meaning underlying this decision? What drives Cara forward despite her fears and doubts?

8. Cara's journey is so long and arduous that she becomes drained. In her sleep, she is reminded of her map. Many people report the experience of awakening refreshed and "with an answer" after a good night's sleep. Why do you think this happens? What is the symbolism of the map?

9. In the ravine, Cara assesses her situation and realizes she needs time to recover before continuing on her journey. She has pushed herself to the point that there is truly no other choice. How is her condition common to many of today's women?

10. Like the expression, "It's all downhill from here," Cara's way begins to feel easier. However, just when she is feeling confident, she finds herself in a "fog" and literally hits the wall. Are these new challenges necessary to the story?

11. Our heroine reaches her goal and will apparently have the help she needs. What do we know about Cara's history that explains her ambivalence about accepting help?

12. Cara enjoys the unconditional acceptance in her relationships with Gaylan and Mira, even though the two women are very different. What are the messages about women's relationships?

13. When Cara realizes that her voice is returning, she decides to remain silent a while longer. With claiming one's voice can also come accountability, expectations and judgment. It will take more time before she is ready to face these. How does this relate to today's women and their feelings about "speaking up"?

14. Leah discloses that Broen's situation in the village became very difficult, and he finally gave up. What do you imagine happened to him after Cara left?

15. As Cara regains her voice, she begins to open up to other women. She sorts through the events of her life as she listens to their stories and shares her own. She reluctantly learns to face conflict and to speak up for herself. Discuss the value of telling our stories. When is this kind of intimacy safe, productive, ill-advised? What do you consider enough or too much of this?

16. Once Cara is healthier and has regained her healing gifts, she becomes aware of an inner restlessness. How do you react to Cara's desire to move on when she has been so happy and thrived so well in this environment? How do impulsions toward change show up in a woman's life? Leah tells Cara that "a quiet, clear prompting of your heart will simply say, 'now' and 'yes.'" Do you think this is so? How can one tell when change is appropriate and when it is not?

17. Leah has made ceremony an integral part of life in the Valley. She invites Cara and the others to pause and reflect deeply upon their lives. How do you react to ritual? Are there events in women's lives that might need to be acknowledged in some way? Discuss the concept of gains and losses at various life stages.

18. Leah instructs Cara to repay her "by becoming the woman you were always meant to be....by becoming a wise woman until the end of your days. That is your destiny." What is she really saying?

19. The journey back across the mountain is arduous, but Cara is in much better shape as she encounters the same obstacles. In what significant ways is she "in better shape"? During the trip, Cara again dreams of the crone. What is your reaction to the dream and the song?

20. Ultimately, Cara finds herself at a crossroads, confused about "home" and afraid of making a mistake. After all her growth in the valley, how do you explain this burst of insecurity? The old crone offers her some advice, but won't tell her what to do. There are a number of themes that can be uncovered in their discussion. For example, consider the time-honored phrase, "Home is where the heart is." How do you feel when you consider that "home" may be a state of mind and spirit and not a particular place? What roles do the "heart" and the "head" play in decision-making? How can you apply the concept that life is about the journey and not about the destination?

21. Why do you think the author does not tell us which choice Cara makes? If you were writing the ending, what would be your own idea of living happily ever after? When facing an important choice, how can a woman find guidance?

22. Our heroine experienced only one of the many ways a woman can "lose her voice." How can this happen? How do you think today's women are recovering their own lost voices?

Printed in the United States
6418